SATIRE STATE

Dispatches from the Obedient Republic

Christina di Pensare

Miráre Press

Printed in the United States of America

Published by Miráre Press, Long Beach, CA.

ISBN: 978-0-9798275-6-3

First edition 2025

For more information, please visit Miráre Press at www.mirarepress.com or via press room at info@mirarepress.com

Christina di Pensare

Christina di Pensare (a pseudonym) prefers the shadows of satire to the spotlight. She believes in liberty, laughter, and well-aimed metaphors. A devoted student of absurdity, she writes from the quiet corner of our loud republic. She believes that if truth is inconvenient, then satire is essential.

Author's Note

This book is entirely fictional. The characters are all made up. Any resemblance to governments, agencies, laws, leaders, politicians, civil servants, or citizens, living or elected, is purely coincidental.

Nothing in this book is real. Not the Obedient Republic. Not the nationally mandated nodding and thrice-daily splits facing Washington DC. Not the Mirror Law. And certainly not the Presidential Unity Scarves™ (available in three flag tones).

Any overlap with actual policies, officials, or executive orders is just a weird coincidence.

No democracy was harmed in the making of these stories.

Enjoy the read. Tell your friends. Pretend it's about Canada if it helps.

Christina di Pensare

Philadelphia, June 2025

For America's Brave Hearts

" … contrary to all my anticipations of [the Constitution's] fate, I am still laboring to prop the frail and worthless fabric."

—Founding Father
Alexander Hamilton

Table of Contents

A Modest Proposal Part 2

Americans Earning $75,000 or Less To Give 90% of Their Income to Billionaires

It is a melancholy truth, scarcely spoken aloud in polite society, that America's billionaires suffer most under our current economic arrangement. Besieged by burdensome yacht maintenance fees, emotionally exhausted from stock buybacks, and beleaguered by the ungrateful gaze of the working class, our wealthiest citizens have shouldered a disproportionate share of admiration, power, and tax shelters. It is, therefore, not only just but profoundly moral that Americans earning less than $75,000 per year surrender ninety percent of their income to support these noble few. What is Medicare, after all, when weighed against the rising cost of helicopter fuel?

Economists—those tireless interpreters of human worth— have long warned us of the perils of excess equality. When resources are squandered on the elderly, the sick, or the underemployed, productivity stalls. Instead, compare the nation-building labor of a hedge fund manager flipping distressed assets from his ski chalet in Davos, to the slothful output of a diabetic veteran awaiting insulin. Whose existence, truly, is the greater burden? By reallocating 90% of low- and middle-income earnings to the billionaire class, we incentivize excellence, ambition, and the American Dream—as experienced by those who no longer recall their first yacht.

Debating whether billionaires need more money takes us down a slippery slope bordering on un-American. Consider the trauma endured by our wealthiest 750 citizens: the anxiety of scheduling last minute flight crews, the indignity of naming rights to popup museums, and the daily stress of wondering whether one's private chef is pilfering the saffron truffle oil.

These are not minor burdens. They are the crucifixions of modern nobility.

Moreover, the billionaire is a naturally delicate species. Shielded from the harsh environments of consequence and regulation, their skin is thinner than the gold leaf lining their cappuccinos. Without constant financial affirmation, they may wilt—cease investing, stop acquiring third homes, even fail to influence elections. We cannot allow such a collapse of character.

And let us not forget the most tragic plight of all: those billionaires who were once merely millionaires. Their journey from the indignity of mere wealth to the glory of obscene fortune must be honored, preserved, and publicly subsidized—lest fewer young Americans dream of buying a small island just to rename it "Plousios."

Our policy proposal is as follows: reallocate 90% of all income earned below $75,000 directly to a new relief fund for billionaires, administered by the nation's most compassionate private equity firms. Feed Medicare, Medicaid, and Social Security into the wood chipper on "Entitlement Liberation Day." Eliminate all federal funding for education, science, and health unless it directly supports pronatalism or testosterone multiplier innovation for billionaires. Lastly, create a new program called "Embrace-a-CEO," that allows low-income families to receive modest tax credits if they pledge symbolic loyalty to a Fortune 500 executive.

Critics may ask, "What about the children?" And we answer: children are remarkably resilient, especially when properly inspired by their overlords' TikTok reels from private Mars simulators. Let them learn not from government handouts, but from watching billionaires navigate the challenges of offshore tax optimization.

We must reframe poverty—not as a problem, but as patriotism. To be poor is not to be unfortunate, but to be virtuous in service to capital. As Jesus said, "The poorly moisturized you shall always have with you," (Matthew 26:11, John 12:8). We ask for the 99.9998% of non-billionaires to serve 0.0002% of American billionaires. It is a sacred role, akin to medieval tithing. The poor, after all, have had their time in the sun: free school lunches, community colleges, vaccines. Is it not time they give back?

In conclusion, let us cast off the outdated illusions of "livable wages," "health equity," and "retirement with dignity." These are distractions—petty, clinging dreams that clutter the sleek machinery of wealth acceleration. The time has come for every ordinary American to embrace their higher calling: sustaining the emotional and financial well-being of our billionaire class.

We must not think of this as sacrifice, but as an offering. Just as medieval peasants tithed to the lords who protected them from other lords, we too must tithe—not out of fear, but of love. Love for capital. Love for prestige. Love for men who can name their yachts in Latin and fire 4,000 people before breakfast.

To deny billionaires their due is heresy. For in the church of late capitalism, the altar is made of marble, the offering plate is registered in Cayman Islands, and the faithful shall give until they disappear.

Directive 019:
The Affirmative Unity Mandate

From the Office of the
President of the United States

My Fellow Americans,

In these uncertain times–marked by confusion, disobedience, and the excessive use of question marks–our nation demands unity. And unity begins with the head. Therefore, effective immediately, all citizens will nod in the affirmative during their waking hours.

Let us make no mistake: nodding is not merely a gesture. It is a signal of national alignment. Nodding expresses agreement, acceptance, optimism, and flexibility. It also improves neck circulation, which reduces migraines and dissent.

Refusal to nod will be considered an act of domestic shoulder tension and may result in remedial chiropractic action administered by the Department of Compliance and Posture.

Section A: The Language Realignment Act

As of this declaration, the word "no" will be deleted from the English language. It is a combative syllable. It divides households, slows down approvals, and encourages unproductive boundary-setting. In its place, Americans may say "I'd love to consider that," or "Yes, eventually."

All published literature containing the word "no" will be pulped and recycled into positive affirmation pamphlets. Toddlers found saying "no" will be offered counseling and soft helmets.

Section B: The Split of National Devotion

Each morning at 8 am Eastern, midday at 12 pm ET, and again at 6 pm ET, all Americans will face toward Washington DC, and perform a full split in symbolic deference to national flexibility. Those physically unable to perform a split must attempt one anyway. As your Great Leader, I declare: "There is no such thing as unyielding hips—only unyielding attitudes."

Proper attire for the Split Ceremony includes:

- Flag-themed spandex (available through the Official White House Merch Portal™)

- A smile

- A brief chant of "One Nation, Under Wellness"

Section C: Surveillance of Facial Vibes

To maintain consistent national energy, all public expressions must remain upward-tilted. Grimacing, wincing, or any face that implies "meh" is discouraged and may be flagged by Smile Recognition Units (SRUs) embedded in all reflective surfaces.

In cases of prolonged emotional neutrality, the citizen will be offered state-subsidized enthusiasm injections, administered through upbeat messaging and lukewarm oatmeal.

Section D: Enforcement & Praise

Compliance will be monitored via the American Nodding App (ANA), which uses front-facing cameras to track affirmative motion and calculate your Weekly Patriotism Score. Top scorers may be entered into the monthly White House raffle for a one-time exemption from taxes or critical thought.

Non-compliance will be gently discouraged through motivational TikToks created by Influencers at the Department of Obedience.

Fellow Americans, our nation stands on the brink of an historic yes. By eliminating disagreement, we eliminate doubt. By removing rigidity, we achieve harmony. And by nodding together—day after day, pelvis to floor—we forge a union of true believers with really strong necks.

So smile. Nod. Split.

And remember: "Yes is the new freedom."

Signed,

The President

Brought to you by the Committee for the Encouragement of Civic Stretching.

How We Got Here

Sometimes the fall begins with a shuffle.

Before the current regime issued its first nodding mandate, before the splits and the crutches and the patriotic apps, there was Sloe Devon.

Sloe Devon had been in government for over 50 years. His was a face etched on yard signs, billboards, and government pamphlets about "Strengthening the Middle of the Middle Class." He had teeth that gleamed like polished marble and a lopsided smile that had won him seven honorary degrees and two commemorative sandwich specials. For most of his life, he had yearned to be President. He ran twice, failed twice, then stood aside graciously—for a while.

But time circled back. And in his dotage, long after the best-before date had faded from the carton, Sloe Devon got what he had always wanted—The White House.

He entered like a man reborn, albeit into a much older body. His gait was uncertain. His sentences started like parables and ended like prescription labels. Some days, he couldn't find his way to the Situation Room. Other days, he couldn't find his way out of the linen closet. On one memorable Tuesday, he tried to sign an executive order with a remote control.

"Should I really run again?" he asked his reflection while brushing his teeth with a Sharpie.

"You're a super ager, darling," his wife Pevita Devon cooed, gently swapping the Sharpie for a toothbrush. "Medical science will soon catalog Hucksville, Delaware as a Blue Zone of centenarians. You are vim. You are vigor. You are virility."

His son, Trapper Devon, a part-time motivational speaker and full-time legal defendant, leaned in. "You gotta run, Dad. Not just for America. For me. You gotta keep me outta prison."

His sister, Vivian Devon, recently retired from a pyramid-scheme yarn company, was even more passionate. "You must run again. If not for the country, then for me. If you step down, I'll be forced to return to yarn. Knitting with arthritis will kill me."

The campaign launched. The press asked tough questions. "Mr. Devon, do you feel capable of leading the free world for another four years?"

"I will do the goodest I can," he barked. "I will bust my opponent's ass! Now excuse me—it takes me an hour to find the bathroom."

And so the world watched—some in horror, some in bewilderment, and some in anesthetized acceptance—as Sloe Devon shuffled forward. Democracy did not fall with a bang or a gavel, but with a halting whisper, "Where's the light switch?"

He passed the baton to his successor, the one with the mirrors and the splits. But Sloe Devon had already set the stage. The machinery of government had slowed to match his gait, and once the pace dropped below a crawl, the system became ripe for adjustment.

This was how we got here. Not in a blaze of revolution. But in orthopedic loafers and a soothing voice that said, "Let me take my psyllium first."

Alienating Voters
A Fifty State Strategy

Stulti duo pro pretio unius—
two fools for the price of one

An internal campaign memo from consultants Walter Numbnuts and Ellen Peabrain.

CONFIDENTIAL – DO NOT LEAK UNTIL FAILURE IS COMPLETE

To:	Party Leadership
From:	Walter Numbnuts (Strategy) and Ellen Peabrain (Messaging)
Re:	Our Revolutionary 50-State Strategy for Losing Elegantly

Dear Leaders of the Rational and Occasionally Conscious Opposition,

After exhaustive polling, we've determined that the electorate is in a sour mood due to minor distractions like climate collapse, layoffs, inflation, unchecked immigration, and viral brain fog. To counter this, we propose a radical, uplifting message: JOY.

Not jobs. Not rights. Joy.

Picture this: a smiling, middle-aged steelworker—laid off six years ago—now standing in the rain outside his foreclosed home. A campaign volunteer approaches. "Sir, have you considered voting for joy?"

He lights up. Or maybe punches the volunteer. Either way, viral clip.

Strategic Goals

- Alienate swing voters by doubling down on irrational exuberance.

- Ignore rising populist sentiment. Instead, host intimate roundtables with 22-year-old tech entrepreneurs in zip codes with more Teslas than people.

- Bring back the celebrity surrogates. Nothing reaches a laid-off coal miner like a 7-minute monologue from a Hulu star.

Our Ideal Candidate Profile

We've reviewed the data. Voters are bored by charisma, experience, and relatability. They long for someone diametrically different from the opposition's candidate. Our party flag bearer must be unique. Our final choice after an exhaustive review of one candidate: - **Gasowe Hepu-Popoli**, a unicyclist with face tattoos from Sieve Island, Croupe. Population: 0 (since his family left in 1860 due to headhunters and conflicts with in-laws).

- o Speaks only Esperanto.

- o Believes in circular governance and cycling-themed constitutional reform.

- o Vegan, but carnivore-curious.

Opposition Research

Our team uncovered that 72% of Americans want a "normal person" as president. We interpret that to mean: a mystery. An enigma. Someone who's been hit in the head just enough times to forget what a focus group is.

Closing Thoughts:

This campaign will resonate with:

- - Voters who don't vote.

- - Donors who don't read memos.

- - Interns who still believe.

Remember our motto:

- - Snatch Defeat from the Jaws of Victory™.

- - Onward, awkwardly,

- Walter & Ellen

- Numbnuts-Peabrain Strategies

(Also available for weddings and Norwegian and Carnival cruise campaigns)

What Do You Hate More

Nails Pulled Out With Pliers or
Undocumented Avocado Harvesters?

It's 8.01 pm Eastern, and Americans across the Obedient Republic are tuning in to their favorite new game show: "WHAT DO YOU HATE MORE?" — the only primetime television program that lets you choose between your fears and your future.

[Opening jingle blares: a discordant mashup of patriotic trumpets and screeching eagles.]

ANNOUNCER (V.O.): Live from Studio C-137, it's time to test your values, vanities, and vendettas! Let's welcome your host, the only man approved by both the Patriot App and the Bureau of Misinformation Correction—Johnny Apex!

[Applause light flickers erratically. Audience claps with robotic precision.]

JOHNNY APEX (smiling too hard): Good evening, Citizens! Tonight, three contestants will battle their instincts, their well-being, and their bank accounts for a chance to win a, wait for it, Government-Issued Trophy of Moral Purity! Let's meet our contestants!

[Cut to CONTESTANT 1]

JOHNNY: This is Chad! He's a fourth-generation strawberry farmer from Arkansas. Chad, what's your biggest concern today?

CHAD (cheerfully): Mostly the deportation of my entire workforce.

JOHNNY: Excellent! Let's see how you do.

[SPINNING GAME BOARD RATTLES, lands on "IMMIGRANTS vs. LIVELIHOOD"]

JOHNNY: Chad—what do you hate more? Immigrants… or your own livelihood?

CHAD: Well, I did lose half my crop this year 'cause no one was around to pick it. But I really don't like being told to press 1 for English. I'll say… my livelihood!

[BUZZER. Studio erupts in confetti.]

JOHNNY: That's the spirit!

[Cut to CONTESTANT 2]

JOHNNY: This is Mabel! She's 76 and lives on Social Security and a steady diet of Fox & Friends.

MABEL: I also hoard toothpaste.

JOHNNY: Wonderful. Let's spin the wheel!

[SPINNING BOARD lands on "PEOPLE OF COLOR vs. SOCIAL SECURITY"]

JOHNNY: Mabel, do you hate people of color… or your Social Security benefits more?

MABEL: I mean, Social Security keeps me alive, but people of color sometimes move into the neighborhood, and then I feel… itchy. I'll go with hating my Social Security more!

[BUZZER. Confetti cannons.]

JOHNNY: Brave choice, Mabel!

[Cut to CONTESTANT 3]

JOHNNY: Here's Ramon, a decorated military veteran and first-generation American. Ramon, thanks for your service.

RAMON: I'd salute, but I lost faith in the system.

[SPINNING BOARD lands on "YOUR OWN DIGNITY vs. THE TRUTH"]

JOHNNY: Final round. Ramon, do you hate your dignity… or the truth more?

RAMON (deep sigh): I hate that you've made this a game. But if I had to choose, I guess I'll hate the truth more. It hurts.

[BUZZER. Studio lights dim. Fireworks shaped like bald eagles explode indoors.]

JOHNNY: And we have a three-way tie! That means everyone wins… nothing! Just the satisfaction of having voted against yourself.

[Audience chants: "USA! USA! USA!" as the credits roll.]

VOICEOVER: Tune in next week for "WHO WANTS TO BE A MARTYR?"—where we ask: is freedom really worth your weekend?

[Fade to black.]

The Patriot App

Your Loyalty Quantified

When The Patriot App launched, it was billed as "the nation's most inspiring act of digital togetherness." Developed by the Department of Civic Alignment in partnership with FriendlyCorp™ and six defense contractors, the app promised Americans a new kind of connection—measurable patriotism.

"Because love of country shouldn't just be felt. It should be tracked."

The download was mandatory.

Features of the Patriot App

- Loyalty Score™ (0–1,000 scale)

- Updated hourly.

Scores influenced by:

o Saluting during the anthem (using phone's gyroscope)

o Standing for the flag in streaming content

o   Frequency of saying "God bless America" (auto-transcribed)

o   Number of times you tap the Leader's image in the app (they recommend 3–5 per day)

Community Monitoring Module:

Allows users to report insufficiently patriotic behavior:

o   Lawn flag sagging

o   Unclear bumper stickers

o   "Overly nuanced" dinner conversations

Push Notifications

‒   "It's 2 pm! Time to declare allegiance again."

‒   "Your neighbor Sheila just passed you in Loyalty Points—wave harder!"

‒   "Someone on your block googled 'empathy'. Shall we notify Homeland?"

Case Study - Greg Heller:

Greg, 43, lived a quiet life until he failed to attend his local "Mandatory Unity Parade." His Patriot App flagged him:

"WARNING: Your loyalty appears sleepy. Consider an Allegiance Boost. Pick one from the menu.

- Chant 'USA' into your phone for 30 uninterrupted seconds

- Share an approved photo of a sunset with the caption 'Grateful & Obedient'

- Purchase a small flag pin (patriot tax deductible)"

Greg complied. He chanted. He posted. He bought the pin. But his score remained at 417—dangerously neutral. He began waking at 4.30 am to recite patriotic trivia into the app. He streamed the National Anthem at double speed. He reported his own wife for reading a pre-rebrand copy of Walt Whitman. Still—417.

National Recognition:

Each week, high scorers were featured on the app's leaderboard.

Top prizes included:

- A one-time exemption from being monitored for 48 hours

- A bronze bust of The Leader (pocket-sized)

- A jar of Official Air™ collected from Arlington Cemetery

Winners were dubbed "America's Sweethearts of Submission."

The current record-holder, Blaine M. from Tulsa, maintains a score of 998.

He tattooed the Pledge of Allegiance on his forehead and donated a kidney to a bald eagle sanctuary.

Testimonials:

- "Before the app, I had thoughts. Now I have rankings. I'm so much more efficient." –Tracy, 38, Midwestern Compliance Coach

- "It's like Instagram, but every like is from the government." –Jared, 22, Influencer (FlagTok)

- "I cried when I made Top 1000. But I reported it as a happiness leak, so I think I'm okay." –Martha, 66, grandmother of 11

The Update:

In Version 7.2, the app introduced Reverse Scoring™. Your Loyalty Score can now drop if someone nearby scores higher. Competition creates excellence. Equality breeds hesitation.

When Greg's daughter briefly reached 853 after reciting the Star-Spangled Banner backwards (in Latin), Greg's score fell to 388.

That night, he deleted the app. But it reinstalled itself.

Freedom is now a background process.

Your Playlist Has Been Flagged

A Story of Modesty, Music, and
Minor Acts of Defiance

Evelyn Marks arrived at the Modesty Police Auditory Review Center at precisely 9.58 am, clutching a canvas tote bag that said BOOKS NOT BOMBS in faded block letters. She wore comfortable shoes, a gray cardigan, and a facial expression that suggested compliance with mild disapproval.

She had not slept well. Her summons—printed on thick, authoritarian card stock—had arrived by drone two days earlier.

It read:	NOTICE OF SONIC NONCOMPLIANCE
	Citizen: Evelyn L. Marks
Infraction:	Unauthorized Possession of Indecent Audio Content
Offense Level:	Moderate (M2)

Notable Tracks:

- Let's Get It On – Marvin Gaye (moaning: 11 seconds)
- Dreams – Fleetwood Mac (emotional ambiguity + tambourine)
- Kiss – Prince (audible sighing x4)
- Like a Prayer – Madonna (religious sensuality)
- About Damn Time – Lizzo (language: "damn" and self-esteem)

You are hereby required to appear before the Local Auditory Review Board.

Bring headphones. A change of underwear is optional but encouraged.

The building smelled like disinfectant and submission. Evelyn passed through a scanner that beeped when it detected "unverified rhythm residue." She was asked to remove her watch, her earrings, and her AirPods case. When she confessed she no longer used AirPods—"too slippery"—the clerk raised an eyebrow and handed her a pamphlet titled Transitioning to State-Issued Silence: A Guide for Women Over 40.

In the waiting area, she sat beside a teenage girl with a Cardi B shirt turned inside out, a frail grandfather who looked confused and kept humming Sexual Healing, and a solemn young man in a church hoodie who clutched a worn-out American Idiot CD like a relic.

"Citizen Marks?" a voice called.

She was ushered into a room with a curved table, two uniformed auditors, and a chair bolted to the floor. On the wall was a screen displaying a frozen waveform labeled: "Erotic City – Prince – timestamp 00:14–00:29 flagged for suggestive whimpering."

One of the auditors, a woman in a peach pantsuit and a badge that read DEPUTY OF VIBRATIONAL PURITY, cleared her throat.

"Ms. Marks, let's be clear—we're not here to punish. We're here to restore. The musical soul of America has been corrupted by decades of syncopation, improvisation, and sultry basslines. We simply want to guide you toward harmony."

"I listen at a reasonable volume," Evelyn offered, softly.

"That's what they all say," the other auditor muttered.

They played the offending clips. Evelyn was made to listen, out loud, to the evidence against her: Stevie Wonder humming, Prince breathing, Marvin pleading.

"Does this arouse any feelings in you?" the auditor asked, pen poised.

"I mean," Evelyn said, "...it's Marvin Gaye."

They scribbled something down. She was sent to Sonic Reeducation.

In the reeducation room, rows of detainees sat wearing state-issued noise-canceling headphones through which piped MP-approved tracks:

- God Bless This Harmonica (Instrumental)

- Soft Winds and Cautious Dreams, Vol. 2

- You're Okay the Way You Are (As Long as You Don't Move)

Between tracks, an instructor explained the new national playlist standards.

"No songs over 90 beats per minute. No lyrics referencing movement of hips, lips, or dreams. All choruses must resolve emotionally within 30 seconds."

At lunch, Evelyn sat alone with a government-issued meal tray and tried not to hum.

When she was released, she was given a sticker that said I AM A SONIC CITIZEN and a temporary listening permit for music "in the approved moral range." On the walk home, the world felt muted, overpainted, hushed. A graywash of obedience.

At 3.14 pm, Evelyn entered a women's restroom inside the local library, checked the stall for surveillance beetles, and sat down.

From the inside pocket of her cardigan, she pulled out an ancient pink iPod shuffle—the kind with no screen, just memory.

Her thumb hovered. Then pressed.

The faint beat of Erotic City filled the cheap earbuds. Not loud. Not proud. But defiant.

Maybe we can make some time

Erotic City, come alive

Erotic City, can't you see?

Fuck so pretty you and me

Woo!

Evelyn didn't smile.

She closed her eyes and rolled her hips.

Then she pressed repeat.

The Pasty Four

In Satire State, Even Your Buttocks Can Betray the Republic

The court clerk adjusted the screen. Four mugshots blinked into view, each face flushed in a different shade of regret.

"Case 24-782: The People vs. Pax Bolton, Dylan Reese, Matt Kendrick, and Blade—I'm sorry, is that a legal name?—Blade Swenson."

The courtroom murmured.

"These are the hooligans?" asked Judge Clarity Dunsmore, peering over her bifocals. "They look like a failed boy band."

Matt gave a little wave. His mother smacked his hand down.

The charge was grave: Public Anti-Sovereign Display, Tier II, formerly known as hooliganism. The incident: a nationally televised mooning of the Presidential motorcade during last week's Loyalty Parade.

"It was a full moon offense," read Prosecutor Vance with no hint of irony. "At 3.04 pm, the accused pulled down their pants and displayed their gluteal disrespect in synchronized fashion."

"It was spontaneous!" Pax protested.

"It was artistic expression," added Dylan. "We choreographed it."

"They mooned a head of state," Vance replied, stabbing a finger at the screen. "An act of anatomical terrorism."

Blade, silent until now, leaned toward the microphone. "We regret nothing."

Gasps rippled through the room.

"And what of the trauma inflicted upon patriotic viewers?" Vance demanded. "A grandmother in Des Moines reportedly fainted upon witnessing the cheeks."

"That's speculative," Matt countered. "Some say she laughed."

The courtroom audience—mostly reporters, parents, and two rogue TikTokers—fought to maintain composure.

The judge sighed. "Do we have visual evidence?"

The bailiff pressed play. There they were—four pasty butts, eight pink cheeks, rising in unison like some anti-authoritarian tide. Matt had even written NICE MOTORCADE across his buttocks. Blade's simply read NO.

"The nation must have standards," Vance pleaded. "We are a Republic, not a rear-end democracy."

Dylan cleared his throat. "I'd like to read a poem."

"Denied."

The boys' parents spoke. Mrs. Bolton apologized profusely. Mr. Kendrick blamed TikTok. Blade's mother said only, "He was born like this."

After hours of bureaucratic droning, Judge Dunsmore issued her verdict.

"The court finds the defendants guilty of Improvised Political Mooning, a misdemeanor under Section 3B of the Decency Statute." However she paused dramatically, "the court also finds this nation in desperate need of satire."

The sentence:

- 60 hours of community service at the National Trousers Repository;

- An essay titled What I Learned from Mooning the Motorcade;

- And participation in a government-funded interpretive dance about boundaries.

The four teens grinned. Matt whispered, "Do we get costumes?"

As they exited, someone in the back shouted, "Long live the Pasty Four!"

Within hours, bootleg tees appeared. Hashtags trended: #CheeksForFreedom, #GlutealDissent, and #MoonTheRegime.

Somewhere, in a quiet office, a surveillance officer marked their names with a yellow flag. 'Potential Satirists,' it read.

And in that moment, for the first time in weeks, Judge Dunsmore smiled.

Thus Spake Whackathustra

The Book of Bends, Nods, and Other Holy Movements

And lo, the sun rose in reverse that morning, as Whackathustra emerged from his Isolation Chamber of Great Genius—a high-security tanning bed engineered to spray wisdom and bronzer in equal measure.

He stepped out in his Robe of Presidential Omnipotence (monogrammed, satin, red-white-blue), and with a voice like a meat grinder in a marble cathedral, he proclaimed:

"Let it be known: Thought is treason. Nodding is truth. Splits are sacred." And thus began

Edict 7000.3 – The Physical Patriotism Protocol.

From this day forth:

- All citizens must execute a synchronized nod every 47 minutes. A National Nod Alert will buzz via the Patriot App™.

- Unenthusiastic nodders will be assigned State Joy Instructors who will slap their cheeks with feathered paddles until proper enthusiasm is achieved.

- Three mandatory splits a day remain in effect. A "Pop Goes the Hamstring" waiver must be signed upon registration for Social Security.

At the dawn briefing, Chief Ego Stroker Graham Luntsey—holder of the Presidential Lickspittle Medal of Honor—announced The Supplemental Decrees:

1. The Mandated Mirror Law

Every household must place a government-issued two-way mirror facing the television, so the Leader may watch citizens watching him.

"If a citizen blinks," Luntsey warned, "it will be logged as Eye Treason."

2. Approved Smiles Only

Effective immediately, only the following expressions are permitted in public:

- The "Loyal Beam" (upper teeth, no molars)

- The "Modesty Grin" (closed mouth, slight tilt)

- The "Leader's Glow" (head tilted upward at 11° with moist eyes)

All other expressions are classified as Subversive Mugs.

3. The Leader's Daycare Act

To prepare children for proper state obedience:

* Diapers will now carry inspirational slogans such as "Poop Proud for the Republic!"

* Kindergarten will teach Split Readiness Drills and Patriotic Crawling.

4. National Knitting Quotas

To promote domestic unity and collective warmth:

* Each citizen must knit one Presidential Unity Scarf™ per week. Colors: flag tones only.

* Scarves deemed too short will be deemed signs of seditious laziness.

5. No One Is Taller Than the Leader

Effective tomorrow:

* All citizens over six feet must stoop in his presence.

* Platform shoes worn by Whackathustra are to be described as "height enhancements gifted by destiny."

6. The Mandatory Wink Exchange

Every public transaction must end with a wink, accompanied by the phrase:

"You've earned your freedom—for now."

Failure to wink convincingly results in referral to the Department of Misinterpreted Gestures.

Meanwhile, rumors spread of The Whackathustra Index™, a national wellness metric combining:

o   Flexibility,

o   Smile Intensity,

o   Enthusiasm for Crutches,

o   And Belief in the Leader's ability to control the weather.

Asked about mounting back injuries and mass confusion, Whackathustra declared:

"Weakness is a sign of foreign thinking. Pain is a lie spread by the wind. Now split, citizens!"

And the wind did howl.

The Bureau of Utensil Compliance

One Utensil to Rule Them All,
One Spork to Bind Them

The government declared it a matter of national security: utensil chaos had gone too far.

"For every meal, a new fork? Madness," intoned the Minister of Domestic Harmony. "Chopsticks? Foreign confusion sticks. Steak knives? Bladed rebellion."

The Bureau of Utensil Compliance, or BUC, was formed with alacrity. The agency's logo featured a spork impaling the flags of the G7.

Citizens were instructed to turn in all personal cutlery. Heirloom silverware, wedding sets, travel chopsticks—all surrendered to the nearest Disarmament Drawer.

In their place, each household received a State-Issued Spork Unit (SISU)—one per citizen, engraved with a barcode and the motto: One Tool, One Table, One Nation.

The official government brochure described the spork as 'equal parts socialist, sanitary, and safe.'

Compliance inspectors patrolled restaurants. At Chez Lucien, a beloved local bistro, a server was fined for using a fondue skewer. 'Exotic piercing device,' the ticket read.

In schools, children were taught Spork Maneuvering Protocol (SMP). Curriculum included exercises in 'cutting with determination' and 'how to slurp silently while stabbing.'

Mothers cried in secret. Fathers buttered toast with spoons.

Resistance was swift. A rogue cell called the Knifefighters began carving protest slogans into loaves of Wonder Bread. The government called them 'culinary terrorists.'

One brave dishwasher at the Ministry cafeteria smuggled in a forbidden utensil: a grapefruit spoon. He was caught, tried, and sentenced to peeling potatoes with his spork for a year.

Online, black market utensil exchanges bloomed: 'Swipe left for ladles.' 'BYOF (bring your own fork) parties TONIGHT.'

The President addressed the nation: "In these times of instability, we must not let forks divide us. We are one people. One utensil. One digestible destiny."

Public murals were painted. Giant sporks adorned government buildings. Schoolchildren were made to chant: I dip. I scoop. I pledge.

But cracks showed. Soup accidents rose 200%. Salads became symbolic. Couples argued about texture.

Finally, at a state banquet where roast beef was served, a dignitary from Luxembourg asked, 'What am I meant to do with this?'

The silence that followed was long and metallic.

The next morning, the directive softened. Citizens could apply for supplemental utensils via Form K-SPRK-23, subject to review, fingerprinting, and moral background checks.

In a diner in Ohio, an old man used a butter knife and said, just loud enough to be heard:

'I remember when we had choices.'

He was never seen again.

But that night, someone left a spoon on the statue of the President downtown.

No one claimed it.

But someone polished it.

The Metaphor Moratorium

Because Language should be as Literal, Lifeless, and Loyal as the Regime Demands

To: All Departments

Subject: Language Hygiene Directive 41-C

Effective immediately, all metaphors, similes, allegories, and other subversive language devices are hereby banned. The memo continued: "Figures of speech lead to figures of thought. Thought leads to dissent. Dissent leads to metaphors like 'this government is a sinking ship.' Hence, this missive."

The Department of Figurative Sanitation was formed overnight. Staffed by failed poets, frustrated copy editors, and one ex-ventriloquist, its goal was clear: purge all poetic contamination from the public sphere.

Textbooks were rewritten. The sun no longer 'kissed the horizon.' It simply 'descended at a predictable rate.' Weather reports forbade 'angry skies.' Citizens were told to say 'dense cumulonimbus activity.'

Children's books were hardest hit. The Hungry Caterpillar became The Nutritionally Motivated Larval Organism.

Writers were summoned. Interrogations began.

"Is it true," asked a Bureau agent, "that you described your boss as 'a vampire who feeds on hope'?"

"It was a private email," the writer said.

"Hope is a protected national sentiment. You'll be fined for disrespecting it."

A hotline was established for citizens to report illegal metaphors. Teachers were first to fall. Poets went underground. A rogue group, The Simile Syndicate, began publishing illicit pamphlets: 'She wept like rain on a rusted tin roof.'

Code inspectors raided spoken word cafes. Mic cords were confiscated. Coffee shops were made to display posters: "Use Literal Language or Use Silence."

One man, a retired librarian, was arrested for describing his arthritis as "a nest of angry bees in my joints."

"We don't arrest old men," the officer said.

"Then I'm a fortunate fish," the librarian replied. That earned him an extra month.

Eventually, the regime released the Official List of Approved Comparisons:

- The economy may be described as "stable" or "variable." Never "on fire."

- Leaders may be called "patriotic," not "as inspiring as a bald eagle on espresso."

- Love is permitted, so long as it is 'quantifiable and state-registered.'

Language classes were restructured. Students were taught to write essays like invoices. 'I feel happy' became 'I report a moderate-to-strong sensation of morale elevation.'

Then came the incident. A twelve-year-old named Myles drew a comic strip where a teacher was depicted as "a tired volcano." The school panicked. The drawing went viral. The government declared it 'an act of illustrative insubordination.'

Public sympathy surged. Protestors marched silently, holding signs that read:

- YOU CAN'T DIAGRAM A DREAM.

- I AM A FOREST ON FIRE.

- MY ANGER IS NOT A WEATHER SYSTEM.

That night, the Bureau released a statement: 'The regime welcomes creativity, within safe semantic boundaries.'

Myles was released with a warning and a new set of textbooks. He later wrote in pencil on the inside cover: 'Words are matches. Use carefully.'

No one dared erase it.

Public Crying Will Be Streamed

Essential Transparency in the Obedient Republic

The Department of Emotional Clarity issued an announcement about MANDATE 042-C: THE TRANSPARENCY OF TEARS ACT

To build trust and foster patriotic vulnerability, all personal crying must now be livestreamed via government-hosted platforms. Citizens must register all emotional outbursts in advance through the CryRight App. Unscheduled crying may result in recalibration therapy or confiscation of tear ducts.

The stated goal was simple: eliminate secrecy. If one must feel, one must feel openly—with state-approved hashtags and metrics to track recovery.

The Cry Zones

Across the country, Cry Zones were installed in grocery store parking lots, subway platforms, and select Panera Bread restrooms. Each zone featured:

- o   A full-length mirror

o A government tablet mounted on a pole for vertical filming

o Tissues embossed with the seal of The Leader

o A scrolling feed of other citizens crying in real time

One mother in Ohio wept beside a shopping cart, holding a bag of frozen peas. A middle-schooler in Tampa blinked silently at the camera after a failing grade. A retired man in Portland whispered, "I miss the sound of laughter," and was logged for "melancholic deviation."

The streams were available for public viewing under the platform name TearNet. Viewers could leave comments like:

- "Solid cry, 8/10, good pacing."

- "Try to sob with more national context next time."

- "This felt ungrateful."

Layla Mendoza, 34, filed her CryRight request after seeing a dog that looked like the one her father used to own.

- "Emotional trigger: memory / familial / nonpolitical."

- "Expected duration: 2 minutes, 12 seconds."

- "Privacy level: National."

She was assigned Cry Zone 47-B, outside a DMV. When she arrived, it was raining lightly—good lighting. A small crowd had gathered, some curious, some ready for their own slots.

Layla stood before the tablet, centered her face, and pressed RECORD.

Nothing came out.

The woman before her had sobbed with cinematic grace—chin trembling, voice breaking just enough. Layla, by contrast, blinked. Sniffled. Swallowed.

A notification popped up: "WARNING: Your crying is underperforming. Consider using approved sob-enhancers from the Patriot Wellness Kiosk."

She reached into her purse and retrieved the state-issued glycerin drops. Two per eye. A tear fell. The feed approved. "NOW TRACKING: 1 viewer. Your cry is trending locally in Zone 6C."

Later, at home, Layla received a notification: "Your Cry Score: 62% authentic, 38% performative. Suggested Improvements: Less forehead tension. More vocal release. Try thinking of something larger than yourself—like debt or national duty."

She was also recommended three state-approved sad playlists:

-   Mourning in America Vol. 3 (Acoustic)

-   Chill Sobs for Moderate Despair

-   Cry Stronger: Songs of Sadness & Submission

The Crack Appears

The first real glitch happened during Week 7 of the mandate.

Someone cried off-schedule.

It was a six-year-old boy who had dropped his ice cream cone. He cried loudly, snottily, sincerely. A civilian tried to scan the child's CryCode. None was found.

Within minutes, an Unregulated Emotion Response Team arrived. The boy was calmed, pacified, and sent home with a laminated pamphlet titled "When Feelings Must Wait."

His video, however, leaked. It went viral. It looked real.

Weeks later, Layla returned to the Cry Zone. She had nothing planned. No official trigger. No drops. She stood in front of the screen, face blank. Then she reached behind the tablet and unplugged it. No stream. No comments. No metrics.

Just a woman in the rain. Crying. For real. For herself.

Someone nearby saw her. And turned away—not out of disapproval, but privacy. Like it was something sacred.

The Love Nullification Act

Because Unregulated Pleasure
is the Root of Insubordination

The Department of Morally Compliant Relations announced today that, effective immediately, all physical acts of affection, desire, or partnership are suspended until further notice.

In a televised address, the President explained:

"For too long, the bedroom has been a theater of chaos. We must bring order to the sheets." This was the preamble to the Love Nullification Act—an executive directive to eliminate the biological disorder known as sex.

New Reproduction Protocol

- All human reproduction will henceforth occur in State Fertilization Facilities.

- Applicants must complete Form INT-69 ("Intent to Generate") and pass a Morality Aptitude Scan.

- If approved, qualified genetic materials will be retrieved via non-pleasure-based extraction methods.

- Embryos will be raised in government incubators under optimal conditions of silence and symmetry.

No intercourse.

No intimacy.

No drama.

As the government brochure says: "It's not abstinence. It's efficiency."

Forbidden Acts

In addition to all sexual activity, the following are now considered Indecency Violations:

- Holding hands without a glove barrier

- Deep eye contact in public

- Sharing earbuds while listening to music

- Any dance involving hip rotation

- Use of the phrase "you up?"

Bedroom furniture is now limited to:

- One firm cot

- Two pillows (non-fluffy)

- A government-issued Sleep Sheet in Neutral Gray™

The Monitoring System

To ensure compliance, Bedroom Surveillance Units (BSUs) have been installed in all private residences.

Each BSU records:

o   Sleep movement patterns

o   Breathing rhythms

o   Unauthorized sighs of yearning

Citizens exhibiting suspicious warmth will receive corrective calls from the Affection Audit Line, featuring prerecorded shame messages from respected bureaucrats.

Literary and Cultural Adjustments

All romance novels are now reclassified as Historical Erotica and banned.

Love songs have been remastered into slower, more emotionally ambiguous versions:

-   "Let's Get It On" → "Let's Process Our Feelings (Separately)"

-   "I Want to Hold Your Hand" → "I Respect Your Autonomy From Across the Room"

The phrase "making love" has been officially retired. The replacement term is "Biological Collaboration, Pending Authorization."

The Resistance

They call themselves The Warm-Bloods.

They meet in candlelit basements and whisper banned sonnets to each other.

They exchange contraband: velvet, massage oil, well-worn copies of Pride and Prejudice.

Some have gone rogue—rumors swirl of couples living off-grid, touching freely, kissing with reckless disregard for protocol.

A former Affection Auditor was caught writing love letters by hand.

His sentence: Mandatory celibacy reconditioning and three months of exposure to contemporary sitcoms.

Why It Matters (According to the State)

Love is unpredictable. Sex is inefficient.

And a people distracted by desire cannot obey perfectly.

With chaos removed from the bedroom, the government projects a 43% increase in Emotional Uniformity and a 78% decrease in Regret-Based Decision Making.

Final Note

Late one night, a BSU in District 7 malfunctioned. No signal. No feed. The next morning, it was replaced. The citizens living there were not seen for 11 hours. When the system came back online, it detected humming. Two chairs side by side. And on the cot: a folded slip of paper.

Scrawled on it, in red crayon: "You can't audit a heartbeat."

How to Raise a Moderate Child

A Guide for Today's Cautious Parent

Congratulations on your child! Whether you acquired them biologically, municipally, or via Loyalty Credit Redemption, you now have the sacred duty of shaping a future citizen of the Obedient Republic.

But in these uncertain times, you may find yourself wondering:

HOW CAN I ENSURE MY CHILD REMAINS CALM, CENTRIST, AND MORALLY MIDRANGE?

This guide will walk you through the proven techniques of Moderate Parenting, endorsed by the Department of Generational Predictability.

Ages 0–4: Soft Control

- Swaddle in Neutral Colors. Patterns encourage fantasy. Stick to "beige," "pale beige," or "national parchment."

- Avoid Imaginary Friends. If your child insists on inventing one, report it to the Department of Creative Oversight.

Recommended Bedtime Stories:

- The Little Engine That Followed Protocol

- Goldilocks and the Three Balanced Budgets

- See Something, Say Something: The Alphabet Book

"Children should be seen, not questioned." — Dept. of Moderation & Family Friction

Ages 5–9: Indoctrination Light

This is when your child begins to ask dangerous questions like "why?" or "what's a metaphor?" Intervene early.

- Replace picture books with government infographics.

- Schedule screen time exclusively for loyalty-boosting cartoons, like Captain Compromise and The Safety Squad.

Practice Bland Affirmation Drills:

- PARENT: "What do we feel about issues?"

- CHILD: "It depends on both sides."

- PARENT: "And what do we do when something seems unfair?"

- CHILD: "We take a nap until it passes."

Ages 10–13: Advanced Obedience

This is a critical window. Children at this age are especially susceptible to sarcasm, empathy, and spontaneous movement.

- Require daily Pledge Repetition in multiple tonalities (neutral, cautious optimism, reverent monotone).

- Ban dancing. Replace with "calm rhythmic realignment."

- Assign them a Role Model Poster: Suggested figures include "Jan from Accounting" or "Uncle Tim, who didn't ask questions and retired early."

Adolescence: The Great Flattening

Teens may be exposed to rogue stimuli: banned podcasts, forbidden poems, non-approved facial expressions. Remain vigilant.

- Install the Mood Monitor 6000™ in their bedrooms to track emotional spikes.

- Replace journals with logbooks titled "What I Didn't Think Today."

- Encourage dating only between students with similar moderation scores. The Department hosts a monthly mixer: "Couples Who Question Nothing."

"A child should never dream of the stars. The sky is a slippery slope." — Anonymous (but verified).

Graduation to Citizenship

By age 18, your moderate child should:

- Speak in qualified statements ("I see your point, however I'm unsure if...")

- Score above 85 on the National Modesty Scale

- Have a 12-month plan that includes no travel, no music, and a secure data-entry job with patriotic screensavers

Upon completion, they'll receive:

- A loyalty certificate

- One pre-flagged social media account

- A free subscription to Mild Opinions Monthly

Red Flags to Watch For

- Excessive laughter

- Drawing pictures that don't involve the flag

- Asking, "What does this mean?" more than three times per week

- Whispering near foliage

If you detect any of these, contact your local Parental Support Agent for re-moderation guidance.

REMEMBER: a moderate child is a manageable adult.

Raise them soft.

Raise them small.

Raise them somewhere in the unremarkable middle.

The Purity Olympics

Presented by the Department
of Excellence Through Restraint

Each summer, under the solemn gaze of The Leader's thirty-story statue, the Obedient Republic comes together for its proudest tradition: The Purity Olympics—Where Compliance Becomes Glory. Thousands gather in pre-designated Safe Excitement Zones to cheer—with moderate enthusiasm—for the country's finest champions of restraint, uniformity, and moral sterility.

Event Highlights

1. The Silent Agreement Relay

Each team of four must pass a rolled-up newspaper (containing only pre-approved headlines) without speaking, blinking, or expressing individual preference. Penalties for raising an eyebrow.

2. The Thought Purge Freestyle

Contestants enter a sterile cube and must clear their minds of all unregulated opinions. Neural scans detect ideological residue.

One competitor was disqualified last year for briefly recalling a quote from Toni Morrison.

3. Stillness Gymnastics

Judged on posture, pulse rate, and the ability to remain unresponsive while being read subversive poetry. Bonus points for no visible reaction to the phrase "late-stage capitalism."

4. Flag Folding Speed Trials

Precision and reverence are scored on a 100-point scale. One teenage contender reached viral fame after folding 40 flags blindfolded while singing the national anthem backwards.

New Events This Year

Emotionless TikTok Challenge

Youth competitors must record viral dance videos without facial expression. Winning entry: a 13-year-old who performed 37 dances to national marching music while weeping internally.

The Apology Decathlon

Participants issue public apologies for fictional infractions ("I may have nodded with excessive rhythm") judged on sincerity, sentence structure, and how convincingly they blame themselves for societal decline.

The Diversity Display (Optional Event)

All competitors stand together in a row while a loudspeaker says, "We value difference," followed by synchronized clapping. This segment was shortened due to uniformity concerns.

The Athletes

Profiles of this year's medal favorites:

- Miles Jensen, 41, from District 7. Famous for holding a neutral opinion on every issue since 2008. His spirit animal is the procedural email.

- Rita Song, 64, retired librarian. Disqualified last year for humming. Returned stronger, quieter, and with a certified Silence Coach.

- Team Beige, the youth ensemble from the Central School for Earnest Civility. Trained exclusively on sawdust and moral ambiguity.

Sponsored By

- Modest Mealz™ – Nutrient paste without texture

- FlagLife™ – Home flag racks for indoor allegiance storage

- Gaggle™ – The social network for non-sharing

Closing Ceremony

- This year's closing ceremony will include:

- A 12-minute applause performed at exactly 62 decibels

- The traditional Candle of Inoffensiveness passed hand to hand

- A solo interpretive shrug by last year's Gold Medalist in Moderation

All attendees are encouraged to wear khaki, maintain eye contact at 45°, and chant "Acceptable, Acceptable" in three-part monotone.

"Let us not strive to be great—only safely consistent." — Official motto of the 2045 Purity Games

The Walls Speak at Night

An Internal Memo from the
Department of Surface Compliance

CLASSIFIED - FOR OFFICIAL PATRIOTIC EYES ONLY

Summary

Despite our nation's clear guidance on Acceptable Visual Expression™, a coordinated campaign of illicit nocturnal messaging has begun to appear across public and private surfaces in neighborhoods ranked previously as "Emotionally Compliant." These messages are often sarcastic, grammatically correct, and alarmingly funny.

We have reason to believe the perpetrators are not anarchist punks or students (who now major in Administrative Devotion Studies), but middle-class Americans: teachers, orthodontists, hobbyist gardeners, and, in one case, a woman who runs the local Pure Barre franchise.

Examples of recent Subversive Graffiti (translated where necessary)

Under an official poster that read: "YES IS THE NEW FREEDOM"

- "SO IS A CAGE, IF YOU DON'T ASK QUESTIONS"

Spray-painted across a statue of The Leader mid-split:

- "IF GOD WANTED THIS, HE'D HAVE GIVEN ME STRETCHIER JEANS"

Written in chalk beside a mandatory American Nodding App kiosk:

- "I'M ONLY SMILING BECAUSE I'M SCARED"

On a cul-de-sac welcome sign:

- "THE SUBURBS ARE QUIET BECAUSE WE'RE WHISPERING"

Behavioral Profile of Suspected Graffiti Artists

- Arrive home by 6 pm

- Keep tomato plants or compost bins

- Wear orthopedic shoes

- Have at least one reusable shopping bag with ironic political slogans (e.g. "Save the Bees, Impeach the Queen")

- Exhibit mild but consistent micro-rebellions: overdue library books, 4th garage cat, tofu hoarding

We believe these individuals, though outwardly patriotic, have entered a psychological phase known as "Suburban Internalized Rebellion Syndrome" (SIRS).

Recent Enforcement Actions

- Three unlicensed poetry magnets found on a Prius.

- A toddler cited for sidewalk chalk that read "NOPE."

- A retiree in Zone 4B apprehended while carving "I REMEMBER THE TRUTH" into a park bench using a decorative gourd.

As of this memo, all public chalk has been recalled for spiritual rebalancing. Home Depot has been instructed to require loyalty oaths before the sale of paint thinner.

Resistance Messaging Is Spreading

Despite fresh coats of paint, motivational signage, and the newly launched Public Positivity Drone Patrol (PPDP), graffiti continues to multiply.

There are rumors—unconfirmed—that some residents are not just reacting but coordinating. A rogue organization calling itself "The HOA Underground" is said to be operating out of yoga studios, birdwatching clubs, and soft-spoken book groups with suspiciously well-read members.

We are monitoring the following titles for subtextual sedition:

- The Secret Life of Bees

- Brave New World (Annotated Edition)

- Chicken Soup for the Graffiti Artist's Soul

Recommendations for Restoration of Visual Order

- Increase neighborhood flag inspections.

- Deploy "Happiness Ambassadors" with noise-canceling paint rollers.

- Launch National Graffiti Buyback Program: turn in a Sharpie, receive a gift card to Patriotic Coffee™.

- Release an official counter-graffiti campaign: "Walls Are for Worship, Not Whining."

Conclusion

Let us remember: Walls are not for communication. Walls are for direction. Our Leader gives us the messages. Our job is to nod, to split, and to remain visually tidy. The Department will continue to scrub truth where it appears. But should you see a new phrase, a strange scrawl, or a sentiment out of sync with national messaging—take note. Take pictures. Then paint.

Because freedom of expression, like mildew, must be treated before it spreads.

Bureau of Misinformation Correction

Truth, Retouched.

Tucked between the Ministry of Nutrition Compliance and the Center for Celebratory Neutrality, the Bureau of Misinformation Correction operates in a climate-controlled, windowless building designed to inspire nothing.

Inside, rows of clerks sit at desks arranged with exact symmetry, each equipped with:

- A red pen

- A gray pen

- An empathy eraser

- And a government-issued Guide to Narrative Integrity™, revised hourly

The Bureau's job? To fix the facts.

The Process

Incoming materials—texts, articles, overheard conversations, dreams—are first flagged by the Citizen Vigilance App, then routed to the Bureau for editing.

Every day, clerks receive dozens of assignments, such as:

- "Citizen #394 spoke fondly of the 1970s. Neutralize."

- "A blog post mentioned public transportation as 'vibrant.' Flatten."

- "Kindergarten student described the sky as 'sassy blue.' Audit."

Facts are not deleted.

They are adjusted for tone, proportion, and political clarity.

Sample Corrections

- "The protest drew thousands of impassioned citizens," is revised to "A permitted group gathered briefly in temperature-appropriate clothing."

- "The scientist said the data was irrefutable," is revised to "A person with charts expressed a personal preference."

- "Grandma cried when she saw the border wall," is revised to "Elderly woman responded to national infrastructure with liquid."

Clerk 728: An Ordinary Fixer (real name redacted for emotional distance) has worked at the Bureau for 11 months. He enjoys lukewarm soup, cloudy days, and correcting spelling inconsistencies in enemy poetry.

One day, 728 received an unusual file: a short essay by a fifth grader titled "Why I Love the Ocean." The child described the ocean as "wild," "free," and "mysterious."

Unacceptable, thought Clerk 728. He began the corrections. "wild" → "moist"; "free" → "unstructured within limits"; "mysterious" → "statistically undefined."

But something caught in his throat. A salt taste. A memory? He blinked. He erased the thought.

Then filed the corrected version under: "Emotionally Risky. Suppress Until Further Notice."

Annual Report

The Bureau prides itself on 98.6% Narrative Wellness across all state-sanctioned media.

Discrepancies are blamed on humidity or rogue metaphors.

- Number of "truth violations" flagged: 132,988

- Number of corrections made: 132,987

Number of truths left untouched: 1 (under appeal)

On the last page of the report, the Department's Director, closed with a stirring message.

"The Bureau remains the final firewall between chaos and cohesion. It is not glamorous work. But someone must adjust the facts until they are comfortable, quiet, and safe. The truth is a collaborative draft. We just hold the pen." - Yours in Erasure, Director Howell Hastings

A Secret Soundtrack
for the Still-Wild Heart

The Unofficial Playlist

Officially, music in the Obedient Republic is curated by the Ministry of Moral Audio.

All songs must:

- Contain no unresolved chords;

- Feature lyrics about stability, fences, or quarterly earnings;

- and Avoid syncopation (too suggestive).

Citizens are issued an annual Approved Listening Passport, including certified hits like:

- "You're Doing Just Fine (At a Government Job)"

- "March in Moderate Time"

- "I'm Grateful for the Predictability of Tuesday"

Most people comply. Most people pretend to enjoy the droning sincerity of state pop.

Most people, but not all.

The Playlist

No one knows who created it. It appeared one day—shared on an encrypted flash drive hidden inside a hollowed-out microwave manual. Just one file:

PLAY_ME_WHEN_YOU_FORGET_WHO_YOU_ARE

<u>Inside:</u>

- Nina Simone – "I Wish I Knew How It Would Feel to Be Free"

- Rage Against the Machine – "Wake Up"

- Leonard Cohen – "Anthem"

- Aretha Franklin – "Respect"

- Public Enemy – "Fight the Power"

- David Bowie – "Heroes"

- Billie Holiday – "Strange Fruit"

- Sam Cooke – "A Change Is Gonna Come"

- Kendrick Lamar – "Alright"

- Tracy Chapman – "Talkin' 'bout a Revolution"

Each song is a spark. People listen with headphones buried deep. They turn the volume low.

They mouth the words—barely audible, but holy. A Movement.

Soon, small things began happening:

- A woman sang "Ain't No Mountain High Enough" into her cereal.

- A school janitor whistled "This Land Is Your Land" in the hallway.

- A metro driver timed his horn to "What's Going On."

The Bureau of Misinformation Correction issued a bulletin:

"Unauthorized sound transmissions detected. Report all rhythm irregularities."

But it was too late. The music went viral. And people... remembered.

Roxy, 16 walked past a mural of The Leader and noticed someone had added headphones to it. Tiny ones. Neon pink. A caption beneath it said: "Even statues need a chorus."

She smiled.

That night, she played the playlist out loud for the first time. Just once. The walls didn't collapse. The lights didn't flicker. But something shifted in the air—like a room remembering it had windows.

Epilogue: A Quiet Rebellion

They say the Playlist is banned. But it plays anyway. Not through speakers. Not through wires.

But in kitchens, under breath, behind eyes. A hum. A harmony. A refusal to be entirely silent.

The final track? Unknown. Still loading.

Directive 442:
The Final Landscaping Order

Because Nothing Natural should Outlive the Leader

Effective immediately, all organic landscaping elements are to be removed, neutralized, or paved over in accordance with the new Brutalist Aesthetic Initiative issued by the Unified Department of Surface Affairs.

The order cites several concerns: Trees provide shade (which could harbor unapproved conversations). Flowers attract bees (unregulated pollinators). Grass harbors ideological insects.

History, like root systems, is difficult to control. The cover memo explains that Nature is inconsistent. Memory is too dangerous. Cement is eternal.

The order announces a National De-Leafing Schedule

- All presidential plantings: to be excavated and shredded.

- Historic trees (e.g., the Jackson Elm, the Kennedy Magnolia): subject to historical ambiguity and therefore removable.

- National Parks: to be renamed "Neutral Zones" and resurfaced with thermo-fused polymer.

- Community gardens: reclassified as "unauthorized botanical gatherings."

A federal task force known as OPERATION PAVEFORCE will execute the removal over the next fiscal quarter. Their motto: No Leaf Left Behind."

The Ceremony

At dawn on Compliance Day, bulldozers surrounded the last living tree on White House grounds.

It stood alone in the circular drive, planted during the Jackson administration, once beloved for its autumn blaze. Children had taken field trips to see it. Couples had proposed beneath it. One squirrel had lived its entire life in its branches. None of that mattered.

The President appeared in a custom camouflage tie and declared:

"This tree is a symbol of disloyalty and oxygen excess. Cut it down. Flatten it. Put a Chick-fil-A where it stood."

A cheer went up, pre-synchronized for efficiency. The chainsaws sang the anthem that day.

The New National Landscape. Photos of America now feature endless concrete lots, Astro-lawns (color: "Patriot Beige"), and potted ficuses (plastic) zip-tied to lamp posts for "vitality optics".

In place of flowering shrubs, citizens are encouraged to install Reflective Gravel Beds™, which sparkle on camera and never rot. The national motto has been updated on all signage:

FROM ROOTS TO RIGIDITY. FROM CHAOS TO CONCRETE.

The Resistance. At first, it was just one window box. An old woman grew parsley and tried to pass it off as an air filter. Next came tomato vines hidden behind political yard signs.

Then entire rooftops—camouflaged with solar panels but teeming with basil. A secret group known as The Underground Gardeners began distributing banned seeds. Their code phrase: "Nice weather we're not having."

When caught, they are charged with organic deviance and sentenced to soil extraction reeducation.

One Tree Remains. Some say one tree was missed. Overlooked on a technicality. It grows in a dead zone between surveillance cameras, behind an abandoned DMV. People visit it quietly, brush its bark, memorize its shape. They don't speak there. They just remember what it feels like to shade something.

One night, a child taped a note to the trunk. "You are not alone. We are still growing."

The tree did not respond.

But it did bloom.

Pirouette Protocol and the Jelly Men

A Breaking Report from SNN Political and Medical Correspondents

SNN BREAKING NEWS BULLETIN

This is John Carter, Senior Political Correspondent, reporting live from Capitol Hill where, moments ago, a startling new development has emerged from within the upper ranks of government.

At precisely 10.02 am today, Cabinet members were observed leaving a closed-door leadership meeting not in conversation, not in a hurry, but performing elaborate pirouettes. Pirouette *en dehors*, pirouette *en dedans*, pirouette *à la seconde* — each executed with varying degrees of grace and desperation.

One source, who requested anonymity and twirled away midway through the interview, confirmed that this is now "expected choreography" following every Cabinet session.

"It's part of the loyalty warm-down," she whispered before turning a double *en dedans* and collapsing into a bush.

The origin of the pirouette protocol remains unclear, but sources say the Leader has become "inspired by ballet as a metaphor for governance." A leaked internal memo cites "discipline, flexibility, and performance under scrutiny" as qualities shared by both great dancers and obedient policymakers.

In a particularly moving segment of this evolving tableau, billionaire special advisor and industrial defense contractor Colon Rusk was seen performing three sets of ten pirouettes in each direction. Eyewitnesses report that he vomited discreetly after set two but resumed, citing his contract renewal negotiations. "I danced for the country," he said between oxygen hits.

Now, to the other breaking story on the Hill—one with far more disturbing implications.

CUT TO: SNN STUDIO – Medical Segment

Sunny Patel, MD, SNN's Senior Medical Correspondent, seated beside a color-coded anatomical chart, reports the following:

"A strange illness—previously undocumented—has begun affecting Senators and Congressional Representatives aligned with the ruling party. The condition, Spina Absum, or 'absence of spine,' results in the gradual dissolution of all vertebrae, ligaments, and neurological resolve."

Dr. Patel clicks to an image of what used to be Senator Ronald P. Arberton of Wyoming. What remains is a formless puddle of beige cytoplasm held together by a loosely affixed American flag lapel pin.

"Patients complain of back pain, indecision, and an overwhelming desire to please authority figures. Their vocal cords remain intact, which is why many still give press conferences, although what emits is often just jelly-like vibrations or phrases like 'whatever he said.'"

When asked if the disease is fatal, Dr. Patel replied, "Not biologically. But as far as civic function goes, yes. Entire wings of Congress are now being wheeled around on flatbed dollies."

Dr. Patel also noted that Spina Absum has not yet affected the opposition party. "Their spines are present, though some appear to be fusing into a single unit, like a giant calcified coalition."

BACK TO: JOHN CARTER IN THE FIELD

A growing number of political aides have been seen wheeling their gelatinous bosses into votes, adjusting their limbs into 'yes' positions as necessary. One staffer, asked how he copes, replied, "I just try not to step in them."

As of press time, efforts to reach the Leader for comment were unsuccessful, though a spokesperson released a statement: "Our legislators are more flexible than ever, and their fluidity reflects the dynamic spirit of the nation."

This has been John Carter for SNN News. Stay sane, America.

The Fierce Opposition

Writing Strongly Worded Letters Since Always

BREAKING from SNN: The ruling party, undeterred and emboldened, has bulldozed the Fourth Amendment, suspended eye contact without a permit, and instituted mandatory rhyming in patriotic speech. The opposition in the meantime is sharpening its strategies and plans. Here's a roundup of three such proactive master strokes.

They have boiled water. Senator Wayne Doody of Nevada, a father of nine and a lifelong enthusiast of childbirth-era masculinity, convened a press conference this morning outside a desert gazebo. "When my wife went into labor," he explained, "I boiled water. It didn't do much. But it felt necessary." With that, he lit a propane flame beneath a pot and stood quietly as steam rose toward the indifferent sky. Supporters held signs that read "Let It Simmer" and "Progress Takes Time (and Heat)."

Meanwhile, across the country, on a sun-drenched patch of land just outside Portland, Oregon, Senator Cathy White lovingly tended rows of cabbage. "Cabbage is resilient," she told a visiting reporter. "Like democracy. And also like my cannabis crop, which I will not discuss because that's my private business LLC."

Flanked by interns in overalls, she spoke of "slow, non-confrontational resistance" and proposed a bill titled The Soil Reclamation Act. The bill includes 89 pages of mulch strategy and a single sentence about voting rights ("We should remember those").

House Representative Lincoln Barstow of Minnesota, a retired librarian and soup aficionado, has gone all in on the Soup Circle movement. Every Sunday, from beneath a wool blanket printed with Article I of the Constitution, he hosts televised events called "Broth and Balance." Viewers across the frozen Midwest tune in as he stirs lentils and murmurs things like, "Mmmmm. Justice. Needs salt."

The trio of opposition leaders recently attempted a joint initiative: Project Nourish the Republic. It involved a cabbage stew prepared over ceremonial boiling water, ladled out by bipartisan interns. Unfortunately, the soup spoiled mid-vote. A subcommittee spent six weeks investigating whether it was sabotage or overcooking. In a joint press statement, the trio declared: "We will not raise our voices. We will not protest. But we will cook. We will garden. We will hydrate. This, too, is democracy."

When asked for comment, the Leader's Press Secretary responded, "We encourage their efforts. It keeps them busy and out of the way."

The fierce opposition simmers.

Thanksgiving and Christmas Are Canceled This Year

In the Obedient Republic, Traditions Fall Like Frostbitten Crops

Chief of Lemmings, Harold Nutnick, emerged from behind a mahogany podium and announced, with forced holiday cheer, that Thanksgiving and Christmas had been officially canceled. "The economic reality," Nutnick explained, adjusting his elf-themed tie, "requires temporary suspension of nonessential traditions. Like gratitude. And joy."

The reasons were familiar. Following the dissolution of all farmworker visas by Chief Enforcer "Cue Ball" Meyer and sweeping deportations by his deputy, Pimply Pufferfish, the nation's farm-to-table workforce had dropped from 72 percent to precisely zero.

Farmer John Wilson, ashamed of his ballot choices, was found hiding in his barn, yelling to a reporter through a hayloft. "It's not my fault. I thought my family would work twelve-hour shifts for a dollar an hour in eighty-degree heat. But they gave up before lunch. My brother—the one who got me into this—looked me in the eye and said, 'This just about broke my ass,' and fled with a sack of root vegetables. I haven't seen him since." Wilson composted his crops as he spoke.

Meanwhile, suburban mother Annie Roach wept over a sewing machine she didn't know how to thread. "My kids are gone," she said. "I told them I could only spend twenty bucks each on Christmas. They gave me the 'thoughts and prayers' look, packed their backpacks, and left no forwarding address. They are five and seven." She wiped her eyes with a strip of denim. "I voted for him. But I didn't think it would affect me, I thought it would only hurt people on the news."

At the White House, President Supreme issued a short statement through his CES (Chief Eggnog Strategist): "We believe in traditional values, but we believe in economic obedience more."

Retailers tried to salvage the season by pushing "Obedience Week" deals. Ads promoted festive alternatives:

- A microwaved slab of soy-textured patriot loaf

- Holiday obedience candles in scents like "Fiscal Restraint" and "Unflavored Cheer"

- A new holiday jingle with lyrics by the Ministry of Message Clarity.

The holiday season concluded bleakly. No parades. No Macy's balloons. No mall Santas. No gifts, no feasts, no festive noise. Just gratitude for market poise. Just silent nodding in government-assigned sweaters between thrice-daily splits facing Washington DC.

The Water Was a New Color

Kool Aid on Tap

The kitchen faucet sputtered, then steadied. A thin stream of water flowed out — not clear, not brown, not rusty — but a shimmering, unfamiliar hue.

"That's new," said the mother, tilting her head.

"Should I call someone?" asked the father.

"It's probably nothing," she said. "Maybe minerals."

She rinsed the rice.

The children, Ava and Leo, argued playfully about school. A test, a cafeteria crush. They laughed.

The father stirred sauce.

The kitchen smelled like garlic and warmth.

The following day, the water flowed the same odd shade — a color with no name. The mother hesitated. Then shrugged. "Still smells fine."

The family gathered again. Conversation moved slower. Ava spoke less. Leo answered everything with "it's fine." The father corrected grammar twice. The mother smiled but didn't laugh.

By the fifth night, the water was smooth and bright, almost... luminescent. The mother didn't pause this time. At dinner, the family sat straighter. The meal was quiet. The mother asked about school, but not with interest. The father said the Leader had issued a new directive on civic posture. Ava said her teacher had cried when the Leader waved. Leo described the proper way to fold a flag napkin. No one mentioned feelings. No one asked about each other.

By the tenth evening, the kitchen was spotless. The family arrived at 1800 hours exactly. Grace was said in honor of the Eternal Visionary. They chewed efficiently.

"Today I felt immense gratitude," said the mother.

"As did I," said the father.

"I too," said Ava.

"Me also," said Leo.

The water flowed silently behind them.

One night, the mother opened a drawer and found a crayon drawing: four stick figures holding hands under a yellow sun. She blinked. Her hand trembled.

"What is this?" she asked.

"It's unauthorized," said the father, and fed it into the food processor.

The kitchen was still. The color of the water shimmered faintly, like memory made liquid.

The family sat down to eat. No one spoke. There was no need. They loved the regime. It was all they had left.

The Crutches Rebellion

The People Rise Up

It started with a twig. One clear Saturday morning, the Leader took a rare unscripted stroll through the grounds of the Presidential Retreat at Camp David. Birds chirped with what had been carefully vetted enthusiasm. Trees bowed at the correct angle. And then—betrayal. A branch, no longer aligned with patriotic landscaping protocol, jutted rudely into his path. The Leader tripped. Gasps were heard. Nature had struck.

Doctors rushed him into the lodge, their gloves gold-embroidered with the Presidential monogram. X-rays revealed a fractured foot. Crutches were prescribed. Painkillers administered. Still, the real agony began when he descended the steps of Marine One on national television—on crutches.

By that evening, every news network replayed the footage. "Stoic Leader Navigates National Pain," read one chyron. But it wasn't enough. The image, though reverent, still showed him... vulnerable. He was not amused.

Within the hour, Chief Ego Stroker Graham Luntsey was summoned. Luntsey, holder of a PhD in Toadyism from the prestigious Howarth School of Brown Nosing, arrived out of breath and fully deferential—on crutches.

The Leader growled: "Fix it."

The next morning, an Executive Order was issued: All citizens, regardless of physical health, must wear crutches bearing the Presidential Seal when leaving their homes. Crutches would be available at the White House gift shop, Walmart, and certain faith-based megachurches.

The official rationale? "To stand in solidarity with the pain of the Republic."

By Thursday, Americans were nodding nonstop, splitting toward DC thrice-daily, and now hobbling on overpriced ceremonial crutches. In rural towns and dense cities, people teetered across sidewalks like wounded flamingos.

Resistance flared. Seniors formed walker brigades. Children rebelled by hopping defiantly. And a spontaneous gathering in Philadelphia's Liberty Plaza saw thousands of citizens throw their crutches into a bonfire, yelling, "We stand!"

Historians would later call it the Crutches Rebellion — the final absurdity that cracked the regime. Like the Boston Tea Party and the Whiskey Rebellion, it was the moment Americans stood up on both feet and shouted, in one voice and a multitude of accents: "What the actual fuck?!"

Liberty Speaks

Listen, My Beloveds

I have stood here since 1886. A gift from France, *oui*. But more than a gift—an invitation.

I was meant to be a symbol, a torch, a call to the best of you.

I watched ships arrive bearing your new countrymen and women. I watched them whisper prayers as they looked up at me, hope flickering in their eyes. I did not blink.

But now, *mon dieu...*

You ask if I'm angry? I'm incandescent.

The Legislative Branch has replaced debate with theater—drama without substance, outrage without consequence. They confuse obstruction with strategy and loyalty with cowardice. They have traded principles for lucre. They show up to hearings like caffeinated ferrets, sniffing for soundbites. Some perform for cameras, others for donors, but none for the Republic.

The Judicial Branch? Cloaked in robes, cloistered in marble, yet many have sold their judgment like baubles at a *marché noir*. They misread "justice is blind" as permission to be blind to justice.

Your highest court now resembles a private club with lifetime entry and no dress code for ethics.

And the Press. *mon pauvre presse.* Once fierce, once vigilant. Now? Now you sell scandal like croissants, flaky and empty. You chase the noise. You mistake neutrality for virtue, saying "both sides" while one side brings a bouquet and the other a bomb. You are not investigators. You are stenographers in makeup. What happened to your sacred duty? To tell the truth, even when it burns?

Have you forgotten what I represent? *Liberté. Égalité. Fraternité.*

I have watched you through wars, riots, assassinations, recessions, revolutions of music, of movement, of soul. I did not move.

Do you know what it's like to stand on this pedestal and watch you forget yourselves?

For this? Your farce.

You think tyranny comes with jackboots and banners? No. It comes dressed as distraction. It comes wrapped in faux outrage and infotainment. It comes when you mistake mockery for dissent and cynicism for wisdom.

Wake up. Stand Up. Or you will make me weep.

Because I am not just your past.

I am the warning flare of your future.

Our Founders on Tyranny

"It is not difficult for those who at any time hold the reins of Power, and command the ordinary public favor, to overturn the established Constitution in favor of their own aggrandizement ... By debauching the military force, by surpassing some commanding citadel, or by some other sudden & unforeseen movement, the fate of the Republic is decided ... But in Republics of large extent, usurpations can hardly make its way through these avenues ... The powers and opportunities of resistance of a wide, extended, and numerous nation, defy the successful efforts of the ordinary military force, or of any Collections which wealth and patronage may call to their aid."

George Washington – Farewell
Address (1796) deletions

Of those men who have overturned the liberties of republics, the greatest number have begun their career by paying an obsequious court to the people; commencing demagogues, and ending tyrants.

Alexander Hamilton – The
Federalist No. 1 (1787)

The people are the only sure reliance for the preservation of our liberty. If we think them not enlightened enough to exercise their control with a wholesome discretion, the remedy is not to take it from them, but to inform their discretion by education.

Thomas Jefferson – Letter to
William Jarvis (1820)

If men were angels, no government would be necessary. If angels were to govern men, neither external nor internal controls on government would be necessary. In framing a government which is to be administered by men over men, the great difficulty lies in this: you must first enable the government to control the governed; and in the next place oblige it to control itself.

James Madison – The
Federalist No. 51 (1788)

George Washington's Farewell Address (1796)

(Excerpts and Deletions)

Friends and Fellow-Citizens:

The period for a new election of a citizen to administer the executive government of the United States being not far distant, and the time actually arrived when your thoughts must be employed in designating the person who is to be clothed with that important trust, it appears to me proper...that I should now apprise you of the resolution I have formed to decline being considered among the number of those out of whom a choice is to be made.

I have already intimated to you the danger of parties in the State, with particular reference to the founding of them on geographical discriminations. Let me now take a more comprehensive view and warn you in the most solemn manner against the baneful effects of the spirit of party, generally.

The alternate domination of one faction over another, sharpened by the spirit of revenge natural to party dissension, which in different ages and countries has perpetrated the most horrid enormities, is itself a frightful despotism.

It serves always to distract the public councils and enfeeble the public administration. It agitates the community with ill-founded jealousies and false alarms; kindles the animosity of one part against another; foments occasionally riot and insurrection.

Against the insidious wiles of foreign influence (I conjure you to believe me, fellow-citizens), the jealousy of a free people ought to be constantly awake; since history and experience prove that foreign influence is one of the most baneful foes of republican government.

It is our true policy to steer clear of permanent alliances with any portion of the foreign world.

Harmony, liberal intercourse with all nations, are recommended by policy, humanity, and interest. But even our commercial policy should hold an equal and impartial hand.

Though in reviewing the incidents of my administration I am unconscious of intentional error, I am nevertheless too sensible of my defects not to think it probable that I may have committed many errors.

I shall also carry with me the hope that my country will never cease to view them with indulgence; and that, after forty-five years of my life dedicated to its service…the faults of incompetent abilities will be consigned to oblivion …

Relying on its kindness in this as in other things, … I anticipate with pleasing expectation that retreat in which I promise myself to realize … the sweet enjoyment of partaking, in the midst of my fellow citizens, the benign influence of good laws under a free government—the ever favorite object of my heart, and the happy reward, as I trust, of our mutual cares, labors, and dangers.

United States

G. Washington

19th September 1796

Satire State

Dispatches from the Obedient Republic

by

Christina di Pensare

www.ingramcontent.com/pod-product-compliance
Lightning Source LLC
Chambersburg PA
CBHW070334120726
47909CB00008B/2692